Summer of Aug

S. Castles

Ukiyoto Publishing

All global publishing rights are held by

Ukiyoto Publishing

Published in 2022

Content Copyright © S. Castles

ISBN 9789360160890

*All rights reserved.
No part of this publication may be reproduced, transmitted, or stored in a retrieval system, in any form by any means, electronic, mechanical, photocopying, recording or otherwise, without the prior permission of the publisher.*

The moral rights of the authors have been asserted.

*This is a work of fiction. Names, characters, businesses, places, events, locales, and incidents are either the products of the author's imagination or used in a fictitious manner. Any resemblance to actual persons, living or dead, or actual events is purely coincidental.
This book is sold subject to the condition that it shall not by way of trade or otherwise, be lent, resold, hired out or otherwise circulated, without the publisher's prior consent, in any form of binding or cover other than that in which it is published.*

To all of us who need a little bit of warmth.

Contents

The Warm Encounter   1

The Searing Chains   13

The End of Dog Days   28

About the Author   38

The Warm Encounter

The squawking of seagulls and the loud horn of a ship woke me up. I got up quickly and folded the cardboard I used as a bed.

"Ranger! Call your friends! You have ten minutes to get ready!" One of the pier personnel told me to inform the other stevedores.

My friends were my age and were either abandoned by their families or forced to work at an early age, making us a close-knit group.

I washed my face in the terminal restrooms. I knew I should have had a bath, but I was in a hurry. Still, I didn't think it mattered whether or not I smelled nice because it wouldn't make me rich. But I was actually hoping it would.

It was 1994, and modernized ships were beginning to appear. However, the ship we were waiting to dock had a wooden hull with wooden balancers covering its sides. Perhaps the owner did not have the budget to modernize because their trading route was only to and from a three-hour-away island. I knew this since I tried to work for them several times and was always turned down. They did not hire me since I did not finish high school.

But I understood it was pointless to feel sorry for not finishing high school. It was simply annoying that every time I hear the ship blow her horn, I was being reminded of it.

"You should have eaten something. You seem fatigued even before you can start working." Al, my best friend, and neighbor jokingly mocked me.

Because he was the reason I had to sleep on the wharf, I simply ignored him. He actually told my parents that I led the gang in beating up another gang from a neighboring community. Although I was among them that night, I did not lead them and was even the first one to run when they started fighting.

When the ship docked safely, people boarded the ship to ask willing passengers if they needed assistance carrying their belongings. Because there was no system in place, the entire disembarking of passengers and luggage appeared chaotic.

However, everyone seemed to be acclimated to it. People and objects did fall overboard on occasion, but it was so rare that I only saw it once in my five years on the wharf.

Two hundred fifty-kilogram rice sacks had to be emptied from the ship. We had to move quickly because she was leaving in two hours. As the passengers disembarked, we were mixed in with them, despite the fact that we were carrying sacks on our backs.

Surprisingly, I was trailing a lady with long black hair, a heavy shoulder bag, and what appeared to be a 25-kilogram bundle of bananas on top of her head. It wasn't unusual for women to carry items, but she became unstable when a strong wave hit the ship. As a result, she took a step back while maintaining her grip on the gangway railings. Perhaps because of the shock, she let go of the railings and concentrated on keeping the sack above her head from slipping off. She fell backward and hit me like a domino, while I leaned back and knocked Al behind me.

"Shit!" Al yelled as the sack of rice he was carrying sank into the waves. He gave me a sidelong glance, but he understood it was accidental. I assisted the lady in getting up and carried the object on top of her head for her.

Al went back to the ship to continue the work, but we were already worried that our pay would be deducted because of that.

"I'm so sorry.", the woman put down the heavy bag on her shoulder.

I was taken aback when I noticed how attractive she was. She looked like a conservative maiden with round eyes, fair white skin, and long black hair. I was stunned by the contrast between her noble demeanor and her not-so-feminine stunt a few moments prior.

"Will you be able to pay for it? I'm sure we will have deductions because of that."

I still asked her if she could pay for what happened since logic told me that her beauty couldn't feed our stomachs.

"I only have twenty-two pesos left. I can't carry these bags while walking, so I will need two pesos for a taxi. Will twenty suffice?"

The guilt on her face was not able to distort the prettiness of it. I didn't know what got into me, but I offered something ridiculous.

"Forty pesos is about the amount of that cargo. How about this: we will take your twenty, and I will take you to your place for those two pesos."

I thought that she lived nearby because the distance for a two-peso taxi fare would be approximately the same going to my district.

But I realized I hadn't considered another interpretation that could be derived from what I stated. She took a little step back and peered around me as if I were a predator.

"I'm sorry. I don't mean any harm. As a sideline, I have a pedal cab outside, hence the offer."

I immediately left, afraid that I'd be reported as a sexual offender. I did not even have the chance to get the money from her.

"What took you so long? Did she make a payment?" Al grumbled as he yanked the sack he had passed to me off my shoulder.

I told him that the lady was poor just like us. But I understood why he was so upset. Unlike my family, who had my father as a regular employee at a well-known wood company, Al had to provide for his sickly mother and two small siblings by himself.

We finally finished unloading all of the stuff after another hour. There were ten of us, and we decided not to discuss the missing goods. Fortunately, despite being aware of what had occurred, the owner did not deduct our wages for labor. He must have learned his lesson the last time he reduced our wages and forced three individuals to quit.

Al and I opted to go home instead of heading directly to another job that was waiting for us that same day.

I did not know what influenced me, but ever since the summer started, which was months ago, I suddenly felt like I had not been leading a good life. We had been talking a lot about finding a stable job but something that happened at the time made the urgency more intense.

When I got home, I saw my mother gambling with horses on a TV screen. My two younger brothers and sister each minded their own lives. My father was at work, so I avoided the customary earful from him.

Our place was situated in an illegal settlement, so we were usually badgered as "squatters" by other people. Due to unsupervised living, a lot of the houses, including ours, did not have a shower room. I knew that I didn't smell good anymore, so I hurriedly picked up a pail and dipper while also readily putting a thumb-sized shampoo on my hair.

I walked to the public hand water pump, which was only a few meters from our house, and waited in line to get water. I removed my shirt as the queue became shorter when I suddenly felt a stare directed at me. I looked up and was astonished to discover that the lady from the wharf was using the pump.

I felt her intense gaze on my body. Just like she did, my eyes made a quick scan of how alluring she was.

I waved at her and she waved back. When she was finished filling two of her buckets, I immediately left mine on the side and offered to help her.

"Don't bother declining because I am stubborn." I held her buckets, not giving her room to decline.

She just cutely chuckled at my act of chivalry, which made my heart skip a beat.

It was at that moment that I knew that I was in big trouble. I might have been a playboy in the eyes of many, but I had never truly experienced the same as I just did—true love at first sight.

"Thanks, I am Vivien." She told me her name but then suddenly remembered that I ran off quickly the last time we spoke, so she wasn't able to get my name or give me money for the incident. "Did you and your friends get in trouble because of that?"

"I'll call you Vivs from now on, okay?" I just smiled at her and acted all cool. "Don't worry about it, it's all good. But lead the way now."

I joked that I could sense a tiger ready to bite if we didn't move. And I didn't smell good at the time, so I didn't want her to faint because of my body odor.

Contrary to my expectations, she actually came closer and smelled me! I have never been more afraid of anything except for that time. I remember saying that I didn't care if I smelled good or bad, but I took it back.

"You don't smell bad. It's a manly scent when sweating."

Shoot! I loved her from that moment on. I swore in the name of all of the saints that I would do anything just to make her fall for me.

"So you are living with Nana and Tata?", my gaze was on her full time and I could see the good looks of the Castros in her.

"Yes. I'm their niece. Are you close to them?", she was surprised too that I knew of her relatives.

"Not exactly. By the way, whatever you hear from other people about me, please don't believe them right away, okay? Some of them might be true but I am not that bad.", I simply put the buckets in front of their door.

"Wait. You did not tell me your name.", she quickly turned around, as if she had forgotten something important.

It was the first time I'd been nervous about giving my name to a lady. It was like treading on a path of thorns, I did not want to mess up and get punctured. "A-Aug Emmanuel."

I told her my true name, but I wouldn't be surprised if she started calling me by one of my aliases after hearing about me later on. But I didn't mind. I believed that a man's past couldn't be escaped.

I quickly left before the people would start spouting things like "I am targeting a new naive girl". But I bet the ones who saw us already did that.

I took a bath. I cleaned my body, almost hoping to have newborn skin. It felt like the first time I ever had a crush on someone. I suddenly had a strong need to look, smell, and feel good.

It was already six in the evening when Al and I went home from our demolition job. My younger brother had already prepared food for us, and I ate in a ravenous manner due to hunger.

The next day, I decided on something that made even my family question my intentions. I wanted to get a stable job. I talked to my father early in the morning before he left for work. He was a strict man, so I did not beat around the bush and told him the reason.

"That girl from the Castros? And here I thought you were changing for your own good. It turns out that you just wanted to impress a girl."

I saw it again—the disappointed look on his face and the regret in his eyes. I did not know how to justify my decision further and just felt my own face twitch. Pressed for time, he just told me to go and apply in the afternoon. Although he felt dissatisfied, I knew that he would rather see me have a decent job to impress someone than continue doing the things that made me the black sheep of the family.

I was immune to the bad things that I was. I knew I just had to move on and work for a better life.

Honestly, I was hoping that my family would be happy with my decision. Was having a woman as a motivation that bad?

I thickened my skin and asked a neighbor to lend me his suit for an interview. The man was initially hesitant, so I had to promise him that I'd treat it as a loan and pay him when I finally got a job.

Just like always, I minded my own business and ditched the tie because I did not know how to make a knot. I did not even bother asking my mom, who was busy with gambling, and my siblings would be out of the choices.

Slicked-back hair, tucked-in white polo, brown slacks and vest, and newly shined shoes were the things I had on. I looked completely different no matter how I checked in the mirror. I initially felt overdressed, but I sure liked how striking the look I had.

I took the path where I would pass by where Vivien was staying. I was not sure if she was around but like I promised – I would take every chance I got to leave a good impression. Unfortunately, even though I deliberately slowed my steps in front of the Castros' house, I did not see her. I was disappointed.

And Dad's words suddenly hit me out of nowhere—
'It turns out that you just wanted to impress a girl.'

I felt my face heat up. At that moment, I understood what Dad was telling me. The instant I got disappointed, the motivation was gone like smoke.

"Hey Marshall, you're looking sharp there! That's good, I heard from your Dad that you will apply for work. Come here."

Tata - Vivien's uncle, called for me, which was out of my expectations. He gave me a small envelope and told me to give that to the man that would interview me. I immediately had an idea as to what it was, but since I was pressed for time, I promised to come back later to talk to him about it.

I suddenly realized that there were people who wanted me to have a good life aside from my family. But I shrugged off all of the disturbing thoughts temporarily and just finished the endeavor I decided for the day. A few hours later, by God's grace, I got accepted and would start the next day as a laborer.

The process was quick and I went back home before lunchtime. I wanted to pass by the Castros' house and thank Tata for his help. As I walked, someone suddenly called for me.

"Aug!"

The familiar voice got me to turn my head around instantly. "Vivs! Where are you headed?", I asked like it was a reflex.

But when I saw Nana warning me with her intense stare, I instantly panicked. Vivien only smiled. She told me that they were going to the market to buy food and supplies. I did not want to melt under Nana's glares so I told them to take care and I would stop by to talk to Tata.

After a few more meters of walking, I arrived at their store then Tata and I talked. He explained that he and my father were batchmates with the recruiter of the company so they put in a good word for me.

I was just about to leave when I remembered something important. The moment I saw Vivien again made me believe that she was my lucky charm. No matter what others thought, my heart and mind had been disarrayed by her since. Hence, I wanted to do it the right way.

"You want to court my niece? Now I understand the sudden change. Well, I don't have an issue with that and I can only wish you good luck."

His response was so confusing that I kept thinking about it while walking to our house. Good luck? Was he being sarcastic?

Not long after, I quickly understood what he meant. Vivien and I started to talk about stuff, getting to know each other. I really needed that good luck because I noticed that my playboy methods did not even move her one bit. Luckily, she was still friendly toward me.

The Searing Chains

One day, on my day off, the searing heat was unforgiving so we went to a café that was known for their dessert – halo-halo.

"You are the eldest of twelve children?! That's… just wow! My father-in-law is truly industrious!", I joked while mixing the ingredients in my cup.

She chuckled and did not want to lose out. "Ranger, Marshal, Rene, Aug, Emman… what are you? A con man? Should I report you to the police?", she actually returned a good one.

As our talks went on, she told me about most of her life back on the island. As for me, the only interesting thing I shared was the origins of those aliases. Ranger – this came to be because I was notorious for shooting games. Marshal – the elders call me this since I was born during the time of Martial Law. Rene – only my parents and relatives call me this and I didn't know where it came from. Aug and Emman came from my legal name which only a few people, usually new friends and acquaintances, call me as.

I was all smiles throughout the day I was with her. I felt like I was like a kid obsessing over a toy treasure as I keep on staring at her. I loved her black hair with a shade of bronze, curly and long. I loved her eyes, gentle but striking. I loved her lips, inviting but immaculate. I just loved being with her, every second of it.

After a few days of talking, I learned a lot about her. Two weeks after our first date, she finally got accepted to work at a newly built department store as a cashier.

After a month of courtship, I finally had to ask the question that I wanted to ask the moment I knew I was in love with her. Luckily, both of our Sundays were free. As planned, around five in the afternoon, I brought her to a place I found untouched in the middle of the chaotic city.

"This is trespassing!" She immediately scolded me for bringing her to private land. I knew it was illegal to trespass but I treated the place as a sanctuary.

"Don't worry, I know the caretaker of this place. The owner is a Japanese businessman that wanted to make this place a spot for lovers. I'm not sure why it wasn't completed but you will understand once you see the view."

After crawling through a hole in the wall, she finally witnessed what I was talking about. The place was an oval shape platform with an open deck. From there, we oversaw the city and it was surrounded by beautiful plants and trees.

I saw how amazed she was by the view. Everything was perfect from the panorama, the timing, and the setting sun. But the spectacular scenery being reflected in her eyes was truly more breathtaking for me than anything else.

We sat on a concrete bench as we continued our romantic date. Thirty minutes passed and all I did was muster the courage to ask her something. Whenever I visualize asking it, images of her rejecting me kept on popping up. But my feelings for her kept me going. I stood up and took a deep breath. I looked at her, staring at her eyes and then at her lips.

"Vivs, can we be exclusive to each other now?"

My question was a shock to her. She took her time which was torture for me.

But the next second, her sweet smile was like medicine calming my raging heart. When I saw her nod, I did not wait for another instant and kissed her lips right away.

From our passionate kiss, till we explored each other's body with our hands, one thing led to another and we did it—we made love, fiery and dreamlike.

I was on cloud nine. Everything felt so surreal. I finally had the girlfriend of my dreams!

It was already 7 PM when we arrived home. I always made sure to bring her back before eight or else she would be in trouble. And when I saw Tata, I gave him a thumbs up which made him click his tongue in defeat.

The summer of '94 felt the best and would remain the best for me. As our relationship got deeper, Vivien and I talked about things in the future like kids and stuff.

The summer would officially end in a month. Luckily, she was not temporarily allowed to go back to the island because as the eldest of 12 siblings, she needed to continue working to help alleviate their living circumstances.

I understood the decision her parents made. It was even favorable for me but I saw that she missed her family. It must be because it was the first time she was away from them for a long time.

One Sunday, I took her to the place where we had our first date. Even though the summertime was almost over, the heat was still raging so it was enjoyable to eat our favorite dessert.

"Dad said that I might be considered for regularization. Once I have extra, I'll visit your family with you. Don't be sad anymore, okay?", I mixed the ingredients for her because she was still pouting.

"Really? I mean you need to help your family as well."

I finally saw a trace of a smile on her pretty face. I assured her that I wouldn't ignore my responsibility to my family and would only act on the promise once there was ample money to spend.

The next day, I woke up feeling sick. Father told me to rest and not to worry about work for the day. Just before lunchtime, my little sister ran to where I was sleeping and said that there was a commotion outside. I scolded her at first but when she mentioned Vivien's name, I got alarmed.

"You are a slut! Ranger is mine! We never broke up. He told me that he needed to find work so that we can have a better life. You are just his pastime, a summer fling, so don't act like he actually loves you!"

I immediately recognized the scandalous shouting. My heart pounded like never before and felt my anger take over me. There were a lot of people encircling them enjoying the ruckus. I ran like I was never sick and got in between them facing Vivien with my guilty eyes.

"Minerva, please go home." I tried to be civil with her because we also had history.

"So you are defending this slut? You are exchanging me for an island girl who acts all innocent? She's just white, but how can you exchange this for that?", she showcased her chest and buttocks like they were treasures.

My head started to hurt. I was not sure if it was because of sickness or being in the middle of a scandal but my vision started to darken.

"Go! Home!" I did not shout. But the people who knew me for a long time understood that I was at the last straw of my patience.

Minerva was one of those people and she left. I glared at the people surrounding us telling them the show had ended. I subconsciously tried to reach on my back to hold Vivien but she actually backed off.

I quickly turned around to explain but I welcomed a crispy slap instead.

"Vivs, let me explain!"

But she went inside her house like she was afraid of being poisoned by my words. Then I saw Nana in the store that had the 'I told you so' face when she saw Vivien.

I did not know what to do and all I could feel was the anger boiling inside of me. But I was not angry at the girls. I was furious at myself because I knew I messed up. My past caught up to me.

I woke up feeling the slight heat from a ray of sunlight. "Mom?" I was shocked to see that my mother was taking care of me. I was confused because the last thing I remembered was waiting in front of Viv's house.

My mother immediately came close and put her hand on my forehead like a concerned hen attending to her chick. She told me that I fainted due to extreme emotional upset and was unconscious for a day. She was afraid that I might have died, so I understood her unusual behavior. I always believed that a person's worth would only be valued in the face of death but it felt odd becoming the recipient.

She was like a different person since that day. She answered all of my questions and I was surprised that she was actually keeping tabs on me. I felt moved. I had resented my parents for a long time. But I guessed my family wasn't as bad as I thought they were.

"Rene, Victor's pretty niece came by and checked on you. She left this letter."

My insides immediately turned sour as I remembered what happened. I quickly opened the letter Mom passed and quickly read it.

Vivien actually left and went back to the island with her father. Her father knew of the scandal she got caught in when he delivered custom-made furniture.

With the letter, she broke up with me. Without hearing my explanation, she deemed it final that I was not good for her. But why did I feel like she was not wrong? It was like I expected that it would happen sooner or later.

I was brokenhearted. Although I wasn't physically sick anymore, it was replaced emotionally. When Dad came home from work, he told me that I needed to go report to work because regularization was on the line.

I simply nodded like it was all I could do. It was a first, being broken-hearted and all. I truly wanted to take the next ship going to the island and see Vivien right away. I missed her. I loved her.

The next day, I came to work with my father. It was the day to announce who was regularized and those to be laid off. Luckily, I was one of those who stayed. But even my father knew that I wasn't that happy of the news.

I was smoking in the designated area when Dad looked for me. He wanted to talk. I immediately put off the lit cigarette I was holding and ran to him.

"Let's have lunch together. Things like this are worth celebrating.", he said something I did not expect, ever.

Maybe I was too readily emotional that I was moved by his gestures. I would be lying if I said that I was okay with the way things were. I was aware that I messed my life up. And I knew that it was because of the results of resenting my family, especially my parents.

We went inside a fine dining restaurant. I was reluctant at first but his reassuring tap on my back told me that it was okay to spend extra for the day.

If Mom knew we ate at such a place, we would surely be reprimanded so we agreed to keep it a secret. A company venture, as we call it.

When the food was served, Dad suddenly asked what was on my mind. He must have noticed I keep on dozing off but it was still very unusual for me to receive such attention from my parents. I told him I was okay. But just like my mother, he was actually aware of my actions.

"That girl of the Castros, you like her that much huh?", he looked at me smiling.

If it wasn't the year 1994, I would have suspected that the man I was talking to was an impostor, a clone, or whatnot. But I kind of liked that he was interested in some stuff in my life.

I nodded while eating a mouthful of crab meat. I thought he would stop there after my silent confirmation but he actually pushed further.

"I can give you money. Do you want to visit the island? I've been there. That place is heaven."

"What are you saying Dad? I don't like to exchange jokes about that matter."

"Who said I'm joking? I'm serious. You can always pay me later."

That was the day that I started to understand my father. I always thought that he was cold toward me but it turned out that he was being reminded of his past mistakes every time he saw me.

"I'm sorry, son. I don't want you to grow more distant as you become older. When you reach my age, you will start to feel the need to be surrounded by familial love. You might have kids any time now and this old man wouldn't want to be a stranger to his grandchildren."

I almost cried. I was sure it wasn't because of the spicy shrimp I was ravaging. From the day they got me back, I thought it was the first time I heard him say something that long and heartfelt.

As we continued talking over lunch, I was enlightened about things I did not know or had a misconception of. I thought they did not want me when they left me to a relative. I resented them because I had to leave my aunt's family because I was treated like I did not belong. I pitied myself while working at fun fairs at a young age. But he told me his regrets. He did not want to justify what happened to me but he thought I wanted to hear the circumstances that led to that past.

I truly wanted to hear them – the reasons. And I saw it, the light in my father's eyes. He must've waited for a long time to be able to say his peace.

'Your mother and I did not abandon you. We were young when we had you. We had challenges – we overcame some while we were still striving with the others.'

He continued to talk while I was trying to ignore the emotional impact his words brought by eating insatiably. From him, I understood the struggle they experienced. Having a kid at a young age without sufficient planning and money became hell for them. As a result, they broke up and I became collateral damage.

The thing that stuck with me the most was what he said about love – *matters of the heart are tricky*. I personally connected with that line. I was not a parent yet so I found it hard to accept that parents could give up on their kids like they did. But I knew blaming my parents was not helping anyone.

Thinking more deeply about my life, the undeniable fact was that they came back for me. It was I who kept my doors closed. Dad was right, the heart might be a tiny body part but it was both dangerous and beautiful. I had my fair share of regrets and most of them were because of the hatred inside my heart.

Dad and I already exceeded the one-hour lunchtime limit but we did not care. As we continued our heartfelt conversation, it ultimately led down to forgiveness.

'Son, I'm sorry for everything you've went through. But I know you turned out great. You might not know this but your siblings look up to you. You might not have a diploma but your sailing in life is admirable. Starting today, I hope you can open up to us.'

I froze. I just felt a warm stream from my eyes down to my cheeks. I was moved by the magic word—*sorry*. At last, someone found the simplest answer to open the old chest that was me.

I immediately wiped my tears with my shoulders. I knew I looked silly but I was too emotional to think straight. My father reached out for my head and softly patted it. I smiled. It must be the realest smile he ever saw on my face as I saw the happiness in his watery eyes.

'Let's stop this cheesy talk Dad. Others might think that one of us is going to die and is saying his farewell.'

Both of us chuckled after that. I became hungry again after all that emotional exchange. Our lunch almost exceeded two hours but we knew there wasn't much to do at work since promotion day was equal to a holiday for everyone.

'Dad, I will take you on with that loan you mentioned.' I said as we walked back to the workplace. He smiled and promised to help me.

The next day, after work, I went to Minerva's place to sort things out. I lied to her in the past because it was a part of who I was. But I didn't want to be that man anymore.

I asked for her forgiveness. I admitted I used her as a contingency. But coming clean wouldn't always be peaceful. I knew she truly cared for me. I might have felt better if she just slapped or hit me but she just ran away crying. Her father came out and warned me to never come close to his daughter anymore. I did not dare look into his eyes in guilt and did not notice that a big fist was aiming for my gut.

Gasp! Cough! The punch was heavy but I wished for it.

'Go home kid. I know that look. You wanted a beating to feel better. No need to thank me.'

I walked away without a hint of anger. In fact, I was surprised that he knew that a part of me just wanted to get hurt and call it even.

The succeeding days, after work, were spent like that. I apologized to three other women like Minerva. I would not be surprised if the word scum was magically tattooed on my forehead because of what I did.

I felt free but miserable. It was like the reflection of my past was all clear to see. I knew mine wasn't the darkest of mistakes but it felt like it. But I had to live with it. The only fortunate thing for me was I had time to change.

I also tried to talk with Tata and Nana trying to get news about Vivien. I truly missed her. I understood why she broke up with me as time passed. I was aware of the stories about me and it would not be surprising that she did too. Although we did not talk about it when we were happily dating, her meeting with Minerva must have confirmed the rumors about me in her head.

But giving up on her never crossed my mind after everything. Even though the time we had been together was short, it was the best thing that happened to me, ever. There were two weeks left before the end of summer. I met the best girl in the hottest season. She was the reason why I had the best adventures and the tastiest dessert. It was all her – the woman who made me a better man.

I did not want to end the season with regrets so I immediately prepared my stuff. With my Dad's help,

I had a five-day leave from work and some pocket money to spend on the island.

Unpredictably, fate played its hands. The day before I get on a ship going to the island, a letter came for me.

As I read the letter, I felt my legs turning soft. I reconfirmed what I just read. She was pregnant! Vivien, she was carrying my child!

I felt a mix of shock, fear, and joy from reading the letter. The thought of Vivien and I holding a little human made me nervous but expectant. But the next parts of the letter just directly stabbed my heart asunder.

She did not want me in their lives. Even though the words I read were emotionless, it was like a magical message that I could clearly hear and see the way she said it.

How could she be so cold? Was her hatred too deep that she wouldn't even give me a chance? Was it retribution? Am I unredeemable anymore?

The End of Dog Days

I ripped the letter into pieces. If I was the Aug before I met Vivien, I knew I would've given up and turned to my 'reserves'. But I changed the day she fell back on that gangway. I was different the second she smiled at me. I was better the moment we had our first kiss.

The time I spent knowing her might not be enough to fully know her. But she loved me and needed me, I knew that much. I did not care about what a stupid letter said anymore. If she wanted me out of her life, I would rather have her say that to my face.

I immediately told my parents about the letter. They were elated to hear of the possibility of having their first grandkid and were naturally supportive. Ultimately, it was up to me to man the hell up. I needed to brave the waters. I was just relieved that my family was backing me up.

The day after, without much preparation, my family came with me to ask the Castros for Vivien's hand in marriage. The ocean was calm and blue but I suddenly felt sick when I saw that the ship was about to dock on the island. It must be because of all the tension and stress that had been built up since the day we broke up.

I took a deep breath and regulated it to calm down. I guessed that it was a totally normal feeling to feel especially since there was tension between me and the person I wanted to visit.

We hired two pedal cabs to Vivien's disctrict and we were dropped off exactly at their house. It was huge and had bamboo fences. It should be expected knowing how big her family was.

I noticed that there were people staring at us, it must be their good neighbors but it was expected as well. I steeled my guts and stood straight in front of the gate of the Castros.

I saw someone, her father, Braulio. I knew it was him because he resembled Tata.

"Sir, good afternoon. Is Vivien here?", I did not stutter but I was stiff.

"Who is asking?", he looked at me and then squinted his eyes when he saw there were people behind me.

"I am Aug Emmanuel, a friend. Can I talk to her for a minute?"

The moment I mentioned my name, he walked away and went inside the house.

A few seconds later I heard her voice. "Father, stop it. I will talk to him."

Vivien's voice made me more nervous than I already was. I noticed the door was opening and closing back and forth like she was stopping her father from going out.

But when the opening in the door was wider and I saw that Mr. Castro was holding a half-moon-shaped knife, I knew why Vivien had to stop her.

Unexpectedly, I did not feel any fear. Instead, I was glad to see that her father was protective of her.

More and more people looked at us the longer we remained standing outside their gate. I looked at my family only to see them picking and eating berries on the tree an arms-length beside us.

I slightly smirked. I thought that my parents must've found it hilarious to see their son in the same situation as them. I knew that their relationship was troublesome as well during their younger years. I sometimes wondered if I received their karma.

"Come in!"

Finally, we were cordially invited by Mrs. Catalina, Vivien's mother. She had her 9th child open the gate for us. My parents and I went inside the house while my three other siblings were outside getting to know Vivien's side as well.

In the living room, there were six of us—Vivien and I with both of our parents.

We sat on sophistically made mahogany furniture opposite each other. My mother immediately told them the intent of our visit.

"So your son, wants to take responsibility for what he did? That should be a given but we don't need him. My daughter doesn't want a problem-man-child.", the cordial Mrs. Catalina just became a tiger instantly. I could see where Vivien got her feistiness from.

I did not want to let them think that I couldn't stand on my own so I was the one who replied.

"Auntie, Uncle, can Vivien and I talk privately for a moment?", I acknowledged that they were protective of their daughter but I told them that there was a misunderstanding between us.

Vivien who was silent for the longest time sighed and finally spoke.

"Explain everything. In front of both of our parents, tell me the truth.", it was short and cold but I felt her calling out to me. "Okay". I planned to tell her everything even if she did not tell me to.

I began with how I was raised unguided and abandoned by my parents, or so I thought for years. Even though I could feel my parents' sadness because of what I said, I had to let everything out—for Vivien and especially for myself.

I went on and admitted some things people said about me but denied those like being a violent gangster or going having sex with every girl I saw.

"I truly love your daughter. She let me see important things that I have ignored for years. She let me feel stuff that I have been numbed for ages."

I looked at Vivien and I knew she felt my honesty. She knew I loved her. And that I missed her.

I told her that the thing with Minerva was truly a mistake. But that was because I thought it wasn't anything serious. I promised her that I already made peace with my past, that I was a better man.

"We are young but we are not stupid. So please, tell me. Did I ever make you feel that I played with you? Did you ever, for a second, feel that I did not love you?"

It was the first time I had said cheesy things for several minutes without feeling cheesy since it was actually heartfelt. I did not care if our parents were around. All I wanted was for Vivien to forgive me and grant me another chance.

As I waited for her response, I lowered my head, and clasped my hands together, my feet were rocking in place, and I swayed back and forth in my seat.

The moment I felt her soft hands holding mine, I shivered. I knew I was forsaken. I knew at that moment I was able to touch her heart.

"Brother Braulio and Sister Catalina, it appears that our children have a lot to talk about.", my father said abruptly, suggesting that they leave us alone for a time.

I did not see their reactions because I was too concentrated on feeling happy with just a touch of Vivien's hand but I knew that there wasn't any tension between our parents.

Even when I noticed that it was only two of us were left inside the living room, I still closed my eyes and felt her hands fearing that it was just wishful daydreaming.

"Aug, I'm sorry."

I broke down. It was not because I deserved to hear that but instead, it felt like it was another way of saying that she re-discovered she loved me as well.

She suddenly cried. I panicked and hurriedly went to her side.

We hugged each other like it was the last time. I felt her shiver as she cried.

"Shhh. Babe, stop crying. Please, you have a human in you now. Shhh. I'm here now. I love you.", I kissed her forehead and we were hugging for the rest of the time till we were called for lunch a few minutes later.

During lunch, Vivien and I cleared up everything. But dining with a lot of people truly felt a refreshing experience.

"Kid, you are the only ugly person in your family. Are you perhaps adopted?"

Mr. Braulio asked me out of nowhere. My siblings almost simultaneously spit out their food and even my parents were surprised by the question.

"Father, don't start it." Vivien immediately protested. I was amused by my soon-to-be father-in-law's attempt to be funny. So I jumped at the opportunity to continue the banter.

"Uncle, you're wise. I have been asking myself that for years especially since they left me with my relatives. Could your nosy neighbor perhaps know the truth?"

Someone spat their food. I didn't know who did but I knew I was a bonafide comic at that time.

I felt so happy and anxious at the same time because it was also that same day that it was decided that we would be having our church wedding on the island a month later.

The next day, my parents went back to the city for work and other things. It was only I and my three siblings who were left to spend the next four days enjoying the island.

The Castros showed hospitality that felt like we were family. After eating breakfast, Vivien and I escaped finding time for ourselves to talk further.

We went to a rock formation that looked like a black cloud stretching twenty meters from the shore to the sea. At the furthermost part, we sat there with our feet partly immersed in water.

Unexpectedly, she pushed me into the water. She jumped right after and chuckled.

"Summer won't be complete if swimming is missing from our activities.", she immediately tried to stretch her shirt because my eyes were immediately glued to her stunning summer body.

As I was too concerned about her pregnancy that I thought that she already had a baby bump or something.

I suddenly had a crazy idea so I took my shirt off. I held her hand guided it to touch my chest and feel my happiness from every beat.

"I know that look." She knew I was thinking something lewd. "Don't move.", she suddenly came closer and hugged me with her hands and feet.

She rested her head on my shoulders and told me to let her enjoy the moment.

After a few minutes, she suddenly stood in front of me and felt my abs. I suddenly had wide eyes when she slid her hand inside my shorts.

We played for a while. I felt like the world that day was supporting our story. It was magically peaceful and warm and we wanted to drown in it.

"I love you, Vivien!", I shouted in joy.

Minutes later after enjoying our swim, we sat back on the rocks and I felt serene the moment I held her hands and gazed at the distant horizon. The gentle summer sunlight that hints the end of the season shining all over the place was so mesmerizing.

"I can't believe it took me this long to visit this beautiful place. I could've met you sooner. I might have been saved, sooner."

I softly said those words while she was resting her head on my shoulder. She did not reply right away, instead, she held my hand by the wrist and placed it on her stomach.

"Just like this rock we are sitting on, it took its time to grow and reach the sea. But it wasn't alone in making this masterpiece. With the constant caress of the waters, it was shaped and they both made something beautiful.

Just like our child in my womb, we shaped and made something beautiful because it was the right time so let's not regret the past but instead be grateful for it."

Her words were warm and heartfelt. I knew that we still had a long way to go but I was thankful that our summer had been passionate and unforgettable, exactly as it should be.

Time passed like a cloud drifting in the skies. Although the summer season was ending, but our love, it was just warming up.

About the Author

S. Castles

S. Castles has spent many years at sea, which has given him plenty of time to write. He currently resides in Manila, a city that never ceases to inspire him. When he isn't monitoring ship machinery or performing normal maintenance, he can generally be found honing his writing skills.

www.ingramcontent.com/pod-product-compliance
Lightning Source LLC
LaVergne TN
LVHW041640070526
838199LV00052B/3475